WORLD'S SCARIEST PLACES

GHOSTLY MANSIONS

ALIX WOOD

Gareth Stevens PUBLISHING

Please visit our website, **www.garethstevens.com**. For a free color catalog of all our high-quality books, call toll free 1-800-542-2595 or fax 1-877-542-2596.

Cataloging-in-Publication Data

Names: Wood, Alix.
Title: Ghostly mansions / Alix Wood.
Description: New York : Gareth Stevens Publishing, 2020.
| Series: World's scariest places | Includes glossary and index.
Identifiers: ISBN 9781538242513 (pbk.) | ISBN 9781538241981
(library bound) | ISBN 9781538242520 (6 pack)
Subjects: LCSH: Haunted houses--Juvenile literature.
| Mansions--Miscellanea--Juvenile literature. | Ghosts--Juvenile literature.
| Haunted places--Juvenile literature.
Classification: LCC BF1475.W64 2020 | DDC 133.1'22--dc23

First Edition

Published in 2020 by
Gareth Stevens Publishing
111 East 14th Street, Suite 349
New York, NY 10003

Produced for Gareth Stevens by Alix Wood Books
Designed by Alix Wood
Editor: Eloise Macgregor

Photo credits:
Cover, 1, 3, 4, 5, 6-7 bottom, 8-9, 13 bottom, 14 top, 15, 16, 17 top and middle, 19, 21, 23, 25, 26 @ Adobe Stock Images; 9 inset © Iain99; 10, 11 @ Aniket Kumar; 12 © Alan Davey; 14 bottom © Sergei Kirillov; 17 bottom © Eadweard Muybridge; 18 © Brian Daniel Leon Machado; 20 © Jonathan Brazil, 22 © maezoe; 27 © Mike Appel, 29 © William Hope; all other images are in the public domain

Printed in the United States of America

CPSIA compliance information: Batch #CS19GS. For further information contact Gareth Stevens, New York, New York at 1-800-542-2595.

Contents

Big, old mansions can look pretty spooky, especially at night. Large houses may have a spooky history, too. Mansions have often been used as hospitals, **asylums**, government buildings, or monasteries. Many people will have lived there, and many will have died there. It is no surprise that some are said to be haunted! Step inside these spooky mansions – if you dare!

Houses can be haunted in all kinds of different ways. Sometimes people may see ghosts, or hear their footsteps and groans. Other times, ghosts may move things around, or open doors and windows. Occasionally, people might actually smell a ghost.

At haunted Cedar Grove Mansion in Mississippi, people smell pipe smoke near the study of the house's long-dead owner.

It can be fun to read spooky stories. But don't get too scared! Houses are happy places, and most people don't even believe in ghosts. No one has ever scientifically proven they exist!

Schönbrunn Palace, Austria

The vast Schönbrunn Palace in Vienna is said to be haunted by three female ghosts. Empress Elisabeth, wife of Emperor Franz Joseph I, was brutally murdered while visiting Switzerland. A palace staff member saw her ghost in her old dressing room. She was standing having her hair combed by a ghostly hairdresser! Franziska Feifalik used to brush Elisabeth's very long hair every day for hours.

THE EMPRESS ELISABETH

The ghost of Elisabeth's husband, Emperor Franz Joseph, is also said to haunt the palace gardens. He was fond of the gardens in his lifetime. He died at Schönbrunn, in a small armchair in his study, in 1916.

A ghostly White Lady has been seen wandering the palace. Who is she? The ghost is said to be one of the Empress Maria Theresa's **ladies-in-waiting**. Maria Wilhemina von Auersperg (left) was forced to marry and leave her job when the empress became jealous of Maria's friendship with her husband. Maria is now believed to haunt the palace.

Ca' Dario, Italy

The beautiful Grand Canal snakes its way through the center of Venice, lined with fantastic palaces. Any of these grand houses would be a dream home—except one of them, Ca' Dario, is believed to be cursed. There has been so much misery connected with Palazzo Dario, it can't just be bad luck. When the original owner died, he left the house to his daughter. A short time later, her husband was murdered. **Distraught**, she killed herself. Their son was killed sometime later in Crete.

In the 1800s, Ca' Dario was bought by an Armenian diamond merchant who lost all his money and died there in poverty. An Englishman bought Ca' Dario, then went broke and killed himself.

THE GRAND CANAL

French poet Henry de Régnier died shortly after visiting the palace. Singer Mario del Monaco was badly injured in a car crash on his way to sign a contract to buy the house. The rock band The Who suffered two deaths from the Ca' Dario curse. Their manager owned Ca' Dario when he fell down stairs at his house in London and died. The band's bass guitarist died of a stroke a week after renting Ca' Dario for a vacation.

There have also been three more suicides, a murder, and a fatal car crash all associated with the house!

CA' DARIO

Malcha Mahal, India

A **derelict** hunting lodge in a forest in Delhi has a very strange ghost story to tell. Princess Wilayat Mahal, one of the last of the royal family of Oudh, was living in a palace in Srinagar that burned down. The government refused to give her back her former palace in Oudh, so she protested by moving her family and dogs into the first-class waiting room of Delhi railway station! They stayed there for seven years. Eventually, in 1985, the government gave her the ruin of Malcha Mahal, and the family moved in.

The ruin of Malcha Mahal had no doors or windows, and no plumbing or electricity. Rain poured through the roof.

Princess Wilayat and her family did not welcome visitors. Their guard dogs would attack anyone who strayed near the property. After being robbed several times, they were allowed to keep weapons, and to shoot anyone who set foot on the land!

A few years after moving to Malcha Mahal, Princess Wilayat killed herself by drinking crushed diamonds. Her daughter later died at the house, followed in 2017 by her son. The old palace is now said to be haunted by an invisible energy that surrounds the place!

Ann Starrett Mansion, Washington

This stunning mansion on a hill overlooking the bay at Port Townsend was built by George Starrett for his wife Ann. The couple, their son Edward, and Edward's **nanny** lived very happily in the house. Ghosts are not always unhappy spirits, and it seems George and Ann both like to revisit the house they loved. On the walls of the house's roof turret, George had hung several portraits of Ann. Once, the top half of her friendly red-haired ghost was seen gazing at her own pictures!

Sunlight shining through the red glass in these turret windows makes Ann's portraits glow a spooky red color!

Edward's nanny appears to have remained at the mansion, too! Her ghost is often seen, and felt, in the house. She haunts her old bedroom. People have seen her reflection staring at them from her wardrobe mirror. Some have seen her gliding up the stairs to her room.

Edward's nanny still seems to enjoy her work, looking after the house and watching people's manners! She has clunked people on the head if they are being rude, and she switches the lights off when people leave a room.

A young couple staying at the mansion noticed a page of their bedside Bible suddenly turn by itself. That's spooky!

The Kremlin, Russia

The Kremlin, Moscow, has been Russia's center of power for centuries. Leaders Ivan the Terrible, Lenin, and Stalin are all said to haunt the buildings, along with many other ghosts.

In the 1500s, Ivan the Terrible ruled Russia. He was cruel. He even brutally killed his own son. His ghost, often surrounded by flames, is said to haunt the Great Bell Tower. Seeing his ghost is thought to be bad luck. Russian ruler Tsar Nicholas II saw Ivan's ghost, and was later murdered.

Ivan the Terrible is said to have kept lists of all the people he **tortured** and killed. To keep his crimes a secret, the monk who helped write the lists is said to have been bricked up with them in the Kremlin walls! The monk's ghost has been spotted silently walking the Kremlin's hallways.

Oddly, Russian leader Vladimir Lenin started haunting the Kremlin before he died! A security chief saw Lenin there, when he was actually in another city. Since his death, people have heard footsteps, paper rustling, and furniture creaking from his sealed apartment, as if someone were still inside.

When a room suddenly feels cold, another feared Russian leader, Joseph Stalin, is said to be haunting the Kremlin.

Lenin's preserved body is on display in this mausoleum outside the Kremlin! Some believe his spirit won't rest until he is buried.

Eden Brown Estate, Nevis

An abandoned ruin on the east side of the beautiful Caribbean island of Nevis was once a fine sugar plantation mansion. The house has been empty for over 150 years, haunted by tragedy. Plantation owner Edward Huggins had a daughter named Julia. She was engaged to be married. On the day of the wedding, the bridegroom and his best man, Julia's brother, had an argument.

It is believed the bridegroom accused Julia's brother of mistreating a slave and threw a drink at him. The two men then decided to fight a **duel**. The men shot at each other, and both died. Both men are believed to haunt the abandoned estate.

Julia was heartbroken after losing both her future husband and her brother. She spent the rest of her life alone. The plantation house fell into disrepair, as local people believed it was haunted.

THE ISLAND OF NEVIS

The ghost of Julia Huggins is said to haunt the house. She has been seen wandering the grounds after dark. The sound of a woman wailing or screaming has also been heard.

Marroquín Palace, Colombia

The Marroquín Palace is said to be haunted by several spirits. It was built for Colombian president José Manuel Marroquín, and has since been a nightclub and an asylum. Ghosts of a nun, old asylum patients, and a woman dressed in black have all been seen at the palace.

The ghost of a tall man in a cape and top hat has been seen crossing the palace courtyard and disappearing into the forest.

The palace is haunted by a ghost known as "La Zancona," which means "long-legged" in Spanish. The tall, ghostly woman in black sits holding what looks like a dead creature in her arms.

Some believe that President Marroquín's dead mother comes to the castle to look for her son. When the president was a child, his mother left the chapel one day to fetch a shawl. She never returned and her shawl was found by a riverbank.

A terrifying headless horseman was said to haunt the palace. His black horse had eyes like burning embers, and a tangled mane that billowed in the wind.

Loftus Hall, Ireland

In 1666, Henry Loftus bought a house in Ireland and set about improving it. He hoped that if he made the house grand enough, perhaps Queen Victoria would visit. She never came, but the Devil apparently did! One stormy night, a ship grounded nearby. A young man arrived at Loftus Hall to ask for shelter. The man stayed at the house for several weeks. In that time, Henry's granddaughter, Anne, fell in love with the stranger.

The area where Loftus Hall now stands is believed to have been sacred to the ancient druids. A castle, and then a hall, were built on the site.

Legend says that while playing cards with the stranger one night, Anne dropped a card under the table. She knelt to pick it up and noticed one of the stranger's feet was a **cloven hoof**!

Anne screamed, and the stranger became a fireball and shot through the ceiling! Anne refused to come out of her bedroom for the rest of her life, and the room where they played cards became haunted by a growling beast and a ghostly woman. The family asked a priest, Thomas Broaders, to help get rid of the evil spirits. His gravestone reads:

> *"Here lies the body of Thomas Broaders,*
> *who did good and prayed for all,*
> *and who* ***banished*** *the devil from Loftus Hall."*

Qiu Mansion, China

In 2010, the center of Shanghai was being **redeveloped**. Construction workers sent to demolish this old mansion house experienced some spooky happenings. Strange cuts appeared on their wrists and ankles that they couldn't explain. The cuts looked like animal bites. The following day, a mason attacked his manager with a hammer, saying that "lizards" made him do it! No one had seen any animals on the site. The scared men refused to return to work.

THE QIU MANSION DURING CONSTRUCTION

Instead of knocking down the haunted Qiu Mansion, the workers carefully moved it, brick by brick, a few yards out of the way instead!

The Qiu Mansion is one of two houses built by brothers Qiu Beishan and Qiu Weiqing. The brothers worked in a German paint factory. When World War I broke out, their German boss left and sold the paint to the brothers at a low price. The price of the paint soared and the brothers became rich. They built themselves two identical mansions surrounded by beautiful gardens.

The brothers bought **exotic** animals. They kept tigers in the garden and crocodiles in the lake! Their spending annoyed the poor people of Shanghai. When the brothers mysteriously disappeared one day, people stole the animals, and sold or ate them!

One mansion was demolished without problems in the 1950s. The remaining mansion is now said to be haunted by the angry animals!

Iulia Hasdeu Castle, Romania

This small castle was built by Romanian historian and writer Bogdan Hasdeu in memory of his beloved daughter, Iulia. Iulia was very bright. She went to France's Sorbonne University at just 16 years old. She spoke seven languages, and was an excellent singer, artist, and pianist. She sadly died of **tuberculosis** when she was just 19.

IULIA HASDEU

Heartbroken, her parents started to try to contact her spirit. In one of these contact sessions, they believed Iulia told them she wanted to build a castle. Her father set about the building project, believing her spirit was guiding him. Iulia apparently said that seven and three were magic numbers, so her father built three towers, three underground rooms, and each staircase had seven steps. He also built a special room in which to communicate with her spirit!

Iulia's spirit is thought to approve of her castle! People have heard ghostly piano music there, and seen her ghost wandering the courtyard in a white dress, clutching daisies.

William Kehoe House, Georgia

In 1842, young William Kehoe and his family sailed from Ireland to America to start a new life. William worked hard and eventually owned his own business. He married and had a mansion built for his large family. Among the Kehoe's ten children were two **inquisitive** twin boys. The twins are said to have died at the house after playing in a fireplace and getting stuck inside the chimney.

The boys are thought to haunt the house. People have heard the sound of children playing when there are no children staying there. Noisy footsteps are heard running around the boys' old second-floor bedrooms.

The Kehoes sold the house in 1930. The mansion is now a bed and breakfast hotel, but stay there at your own risk! You may bump into Mr. Kehoe, who likes to wander around and unlock the entrance doors; or meet Mrs. Kehoe, who sometimes sits on the end of guests' beds!

Famous New York Jets football player Joe Namath once owned this haunted house.

WILLIAM KEHOE HOUSE

Borley Rectory, England

Once known as the most haunted house in England, Borley Rectory had its share of ghosts! When Eric Smith and his wife lived in the house, they experienced so many strange events that a **paranormal** expert, Harry Price, stayed there for a year to study it! In his report, he told of mysterious footsteps and servants' bells ringing all by themselves.

The couple sold the house to Reverend Foyster, his wife Marianne, and daughter Adelaide. They experienced windows breaking mysteriously and strange messages on the walls appearing and then disappearing. Marianne was once thrown from her bed!

Paranormal expert Harry Price (left) was accused of faking research at the house. A visiting reporter was hit on the head by a pebble supposedly thrown by a ghost. The reporter searched Price's coat pockets and found they were filled with stones!

One of Price's helpers, Louis Mayerling, later admitted many hauntings were **hoaxes**. However, Mayerling believed one strange event, as he actually lost the sight in one eye after a bright flash during a **séance.**

One of the rectory's owners, Reverend Harry Bull, had 14 children who enjoyed tricking people. His six-year-old made the piano seem to play by itself by plucking the strings with a poker while hiding in a gap in the wall. Servants' bells were rung by poking them with a stick through a barred window in the kitchen hallway.

The writing that appeared and disappeared on the rectory walls is now thought to have vanished because the walls were damp.

Glossary

asylums institutions for the care of those unable to care for themselves, especially for the insane

banished driven away

cloven hoof a foot like a goat's, with the front part divided into two parts

derelict abandoned by the owner

distraught disturbed by painful feelings

duel an arranged contest between two people with deadly weapons in order to settle a point of honor

exotic introduced from another country

hoaxes acts intended to trick

inquisitive curious

ladies-in-waiting female assistants attending a royal or high-ranking noblewoman

mausoleum a large tomb

nanny a person, typically a woman, employed to look after a child in its home

paranormal events impossible to explain by known natural forces or by science

redeveloped rebuilt

séance a meeting to communicate with spirits

tortured to be punished or forced to do or say something by causing great pain

tuberculosis a disease often affecting the lungs

Further Reading

Owings, Lisa. *Haunted Houses (Blastoff Discovery: Investigating the Unexplained)*. New York, NY: Blastoff! Discovery, 2018.

Williams, Dinah. *Dark Mansions (Scary Places)*. New York, NY: Bearport Publishing, 2016.

Website

Wonderopolis page discussing if ghosts are real
https://wonderopolis.org/wonder/are-ghosts-real

Publisher's note to educators and parents:
Our editors have carefully reviewed these websites to ensure that they are suitable for students. Many websites change frequently, however, and we cannot guarantee that a site's future contents will continue to meet our high standards of quality and educational value. Be advised that students should be closely supervised whenever they access the Internet.

Index